The
Faithful Gardener

ALSO BY CLARISSA PINKOLA ESTÉS, PH.D.

Women Who Run with the Wolves

The Gift of Story

The
Faithful
Gardener

A Wise Tale
About That Which
Can Never Die

Clarissa Pinkola Estés, Ph.D.

London   Sydney   Auckland   Johannesburg

1 3 5 7 9 10 8 6 4 2

First published in 1995 by HarperCollinsSanFrancisco, a division of HarperCollinsPublishers

This edition published in 1996 by Rider,
an imprint of Ebury Press
Random House, 20 Vauxhall Bridge Road, London SW1V 2SA

Random House Australia (Pty) Limited
20 Alfred Street, Milsons Point, Sydney,
New South Wales 2061, Australia

Random House New Zealand Limited
18 Poland Road, Glenfield
Auckland 10, New Zealand

Random House South Africa (Pty) Limited
PO Box 337, Bergvlei, South Africa

Random House UK Limited Reg. No. 954009

Illustrations by Kathleen Edwards

Papers used by Rider Books are natural, recyclable products made from wood grown in sustainable forests. In addition, the paper in this book is acid-free/recycled/chlorine free

Printed by R. R. Donnelley and Sons, Inc.

A CIP catalogue record for this book is available from the British Library

ISBN 0–7126–7211–7

New seed
is faithful.
It roots deepest
in the places
that are
most empty.

C. P. ESTÉS

A drága clodoknek. Sokan nincsenek
már kozottunk, de szibunknrn
még mindig élnek.

y

Por los deportados y emigrantes
de mi familia que han cruzado
el río, otra vez y otra vez,
en dos direcciones, con sus
sombreros y sus corazones
en sus manos.

y

To the faithful fourteen
of Storm King Mountain,
who gave their lives
for love of people and the forest.

They shall all live forever.

Contents

The Blessing

We
have an old family
blessing:
"Whomsoever is still awake at the end
of a night of stories, will surely
become the wisest person in the world." So may it be
for
you.
So may it be
for us all.

C. P. ESTÉS

The
Faithful Gardener

WITHIN THIS SMALL BOOK THERE ARE SEVERAL stories. Like *Matriochka* dolls, they fit one inside the other.

Among my people, both Magyar and *Mexicano,* we have long traditions of telling stories while we work at our daily labors. Questions about the living of life, especially those pertaining to matters of heart and soul, are most often answered by telling a story or a series of tales. We consider story our living relative, and so it seems to us completely sensible that as one friend invites another friend to join in the conversation, so, too, a certain story calls forth a specific second story, which in turn evokes a third story, and frequently a fourth and a fifth, and occasionally several more, until the answer to a single question has become several stories long.[1]

So, according to our rustic practices you can see why, before I tell you this singular story about *That Which Can Never Die,* I must first tell you the story of my uncle, an old peasant farmer who survived the horrors of World War II in Hungary. He brought the essence of this story through burning forests, through memories of unutterable events of days and nights in slave labor camps. He brought the seed of this story over oceans in the dark of steerage to America. He sheltered this story as he rode black trains through the golden fields along the northern border that separates Canada from the United States. Through all this and much more, he held the spirit of the story in a refuge near his heart, somehow managing to hold it safely away from the wars crackling inside him.

But even before I tell Uncle's story, I must tell you the story he told me about "This Man," the old farmer he knew in the old country who attempted to defend a young and precious grove of trees from being destroyed by a marauding foreign army.

However, in order to tell you the story of "This Man," I must first tell you a story about how stories were created to begin with, for without the creation of stories, there would be no stories to tell at all—no story about stories, no story about my uncle, no story about "This Man," and no story about *That Which Can Never Die*—and the rest of the pages of this book would remain as unwritten upon as the autumn moon.

In my family, the old ones practiced a tradition called "make-story," this being a time—often over a meal rich in aromas of fresh onions, warm bread, and spicy rice-sausage—when the elders encouraged the young to weave tales, poems, and other pieces. The old ones laughed with one another as they ate. To us they said, "We are going to test you to see if you are gaining any knowledge worth having. Come, come now, give us a story from scratch. Let us see you flex your story muscles."

This story about stories was one of the first I wove as a young child.[2]

The Creation of Stories

How did stories come into being?[3] Ah, stories came into the world because God was lonely.

God was lonely? Oh, yes, for you see, the void at the beginning of time was very dark. The void was dark because it was so tightly packed with stories that not even one story stood out from the others.

Stories were therefore without form, and the face of God moved over the deep, searching and searching—for a story. And God's loneliness was very great.

Finally, a great idea rose up, and God whispered, "Let there be light."

And there was light so great that God was able to reach into the void and separate the dark stories from the stories of light. As a result, clear morning stories came to life, and fine evening tales as well. And God saw that it was good.

Now God felt encouraged, and next separated the heavenly stories from the earthly stories, and these from the stories about water. Then God took great joy in creating the small and the tall trees and brilliantly colored seeds and plants, so that there could be stories about the trees and seeds, and plants, too.

God laughed with pleasure, and from God's laughter fell the stars and the sky into their places. God set into the sky the golden light, the sun, to rule the day, and the moon, the silver light, to rule the night. And in all, God created these so that there would be stories about the stars and the moon, stories about the sun, and stories about all the mysteries of night.

God was so pleased with these that God turned to creating birds, sea monsters, and every living creature that moves, every fish and all the plants under the sea, and every winged creature, and all the cattle and creeping things, and all the beasts of the earth, according to their kind. And from all these came stories about God's winged messengers, and stories about ghosts and monsters, and tales of whales and fishes, and other stories about life before life knew itself, about all that had life now, and all that would come to life one day.

Yet even with all these wondrous creatures and all these magnificent stories, even with all the pleasures of creating, God was still lonely.

God paced and thought, and thought and paced, and finally! it came to our great Creator. "Ah. Let us make human beings in our image, after our likeness. Let them care for, and be cared for in return, by all creatures of the seas, all those of the air, and all those of the earth."

So God created human beings from the dust of the ground, and breathed into their nostrils the breath of life, and human beings became living souls: male and female God created them. And as these were created, suddenly, all the stories that go along with being completely human also sprang to life, millions and millions of stories. And God blessed all of these, and placed them in a garden called Eden.

Now God strode through the heavens wreathed in smiles, for at last, you see, God was lonely no more.

It was not stories that had been missing
from creation, but rather, and most especially,
the soulful humans who could tell them.

Now surely, amongst the most soulful humans ever created, especially those mad for stories, hard work, and
the living of life, were the dancing fools, wise old crows,
grumpy sages, and "almost saints" who made up the old
people in our family.

The included my uncle, who, whenever I told "The
Creation of Stories," shouted afterward, "Listen, my
friends, to what this child has said. Do we not believe
in a God who loves stories? But for us then, God would
be lonely! We must not let God down—so a story now,
another story!" And we went on with our work and
our stories; sometimes all day and hard into the night
we would go on.

The one who called for another story the way one
might call for more dark ale—that was my uncle whom
I called Zovár,[4] for whenever he had a few pennies, he
bought himself a big, loosely rolled cigar. He took great

pleasure in trying to smoke it before its light went out for the thousandth time.

Uncle was a relative of my foster family, an old farmer who, one evening at dusk in Hungary during World War II, had been dragged from his small farmhouse and had somehow managed, as he said, "through divine forces that no one understands," to stay alive after being taken off to be worked and starved to death in a slave labor camp far away at the Russian border.

Back then when I was growing up, every time someone said—as news commentators on the radio, and strangers on the road sometimes did—"Nazi Germany did this, the Deutchlanders did that," Uncle gave the same quiet counsel: "You are mistaken. The Nazis and their helpers were not from Germany. *Gyáva népnek nincs hazája.* Cowards have no country of their own. Those demons were from hell."

After a long time the war in Europe had raged itself out.[5] My foster father, with help from the Red Cross and the underground workers, searched the refugee camps, finally finding our old uncle, and later several other elderly relatives. My foster father helped all be released from the camps in which they were held. But to find a port to sail from, the refugees had to crisscross Europe by foot, by cart, and by lorry until, with many inspections of papers, and much fearful waiting, they could struggle up a gangplank into the belly of a great ship bound for "Ahmer-ee-kha," America.

There were no phones on either side of the great ocean, no way to tell where was whom and when. Everyone's fate was held in the hands of strangers: farmers, and families along the roads, underground holy men, brave nuns, and nurses in tiny outposts—all of whom, in our family, we still refer to as "the blessed."

For three weeks in the dark, Uncle came across the ocean. Thence, in a sweltering summer, he journeyed across half the northern border of the United States by teeming train, the air steaming by day and suffocating by night.

Finally, notice of Uncle's arrival was sent to us in the form of a telegram with no message typed upon it. The financially poor refugee organizations had arranged to send a blank telegram the day before the refugee was to arrive at the appointed place. So, we knew that Uncle's train would arrive some time the next day at what had been designated "Refugee Depot," the great rail station in Chicago, one hundred miles to the west of our rural village.

I was five years old the day we boarded the railway to go gather Uncle up. We rode for three hours to the west. The train stopped at every orchard lift and wooden crate platform along the way. We took along enough family members to be counted as a small sovereign nation. We carried enough bread, cheese, bags, boxes, and bottles of water, homemade beer and wine, and warm seltzer to feed and water ourselves and fifty other families, should the opportunity arise.

Squeezed together like canned plums in a pint-sized glass jar, we rode the interminably hot train all the way to Chicago. Yet we were filled fresh with longing, hope, and excitement to find our war-torn family member and to bring him home at last.

THE WAIT FOR UNCLE'S TRAIN WAS VERY LONG. In that great iron-raftered grotto they called a railway station, we waited throughout the afternoon, then past evening, and finally far into the night—all in a heat that withered flowers, clothing, and humans.

The great mass of humanity thronging there was further confused by the fact that the loudspeakers announcing track numbers for train arrivals so echoed in such great peals that no one could make out what was being said. The platforms shook and shuddered with each train's arrival. The sounds of iron brakes screaming down on iron wheels, the enormous loud clankings and great hissings, the smells of oils from the engine stacks and from the kerosene in the railmen's swinging lanterns—all these were profound.

The trains were made of blackened steel and iron. They were put together with what seemed like hundreds of perfectly machined wheels, both large and small, and thousands and thousands of rivets all around. A beautiful gold writing was outlined with red on every railcar all the way down the line.

The engines stood three times higher than the tallest man. The heat from just one of the trains felt like the blast of twenty-five armored furnaces tied one to the next by giant cleats. People sagged against the railway station pillars, and without an ounce of exertion, they, as my foster father put it, "schvet like elephants."

From my point of view as a child, everything was all elbows, stomachs and rear ends, all shoulders, cranings of necks, men's stained shirts, women in cocked hats with feathers wobbling, and high heels that looked like deer hooves. There were women in babushkas with unshaven legs and arms, and shrunken bellies, and men in black suits made gray by smoke and ash. There were many old people so bent over that their size was more equal to mine. I could meet directly the eyes of many old ones, and they smiled at me with the most alarmingly toothless, but ever so kindly, smiles.

Crowds gathered around one door or another all down the long rows of railcars. I had never seen so many grown-ups crying, dancing jigs, laughing, back slapping, cackling, and calling out all at once. People thronged, and tears were everywhere overlaid with the smells of garlic, whiskey, and perspiration. And the fog of the humid night, and the steam from the great engines hovered in a huge nimbus around the entire scene.

Suddenly, the ever-moving jumble of herringbones and solids, plaids and polka dots parted, and far down the platform, in a lonely space all his own, stood a bewildered old man dressed in ragged peasant garb. He was haloed behind by the great railway lights in wire cages.

From the look on my foster father's face, I knew this was the soul we were seeking. For a moment, Father's face lost all expression entirely, and then he leaped —yes, *leaped,* I am certain that my tall father leaped— across the dozens of baggage carts, and shouldered his way upstream through waves of humanity in order to finally throw his arms about this one gaunt and towering man.

My father directed poor Uncle across the platform, holding him around the shoulders and guiding him by the elbow as well, bringing him through the crowd.

"This! This is your uncle!" my father cried as though he had just won every bounty worth winning in the entire universe.

Uncle was a huge man up close, like a giant from fairy tales come to life. He wore a wilted white shirt with no collar or cuffs and long baggy pantaloons so wide they seemed like a full skirt that hung all the way to the ground. His raw, red forearms were knotted with broad muscles. I had to bend my head way back in order to see his face. He had mustachios from cheek to cheek, and I could smell every foreignness on him, from the sheep's wool of his misshapen knitted shoes[6] to something like lake water in his hair.

Uncle set down his little sack of goods and his cardboard suitcase. He slowly took off his hat and knelt before me right there on the concrete walkway. Many shoes and boots hurried around us. I saw the sweat-soaked silver hairs of his sideburns, and the fluorescent silver bristles on his chin and cheeks. Uncle reached out and held my head with one big hand and put his other arm around my body. I will never forget his words as he hugged me close to him: "A . . . living . . . child . . . ," he whispered.

Although shy of strangers, I embraced him whole-heartedly in return, for though I knew no words to describe it then, I understood the look in his eyes. It was a look I had already seen once before in my young life, having seen the eyes of horses who had survived a swift and terrible stable fire.

THIS NEWLY FOUND GIANT UNCLE CAME HOME with us. I learned that he was a man of much solitude. I discovered also that even when he took his cigar out of his mouth, one side of his lip was higher than the other and his mouth would not close evenly. "This is what comes from smoking cigars as a little boy," he said, and then laughed. "Don't you smoke cigars, and then your pretty little mouth will not look like mine when you grow up."

I loved this uncle, even though his front teeth were gray when he smiled. He had dark and scary molars in the back of his mouth. His unusually broad brow was marked with astonishing eyebrows that were like wire brushes shaped into wings that hung out over his eyes like visors. His hands could hold five pheasant necks at once. Best of all were his light eyes. In direct sunlight, they seemed the color of a warm and true molten gold.

Uncle had only a second-grade education, and he lived in the new country as he had lived in the old country —as a man who could mend a harness but could not repair anything that had parts driven by electricity, a man who could drive an ox but not a car, one who had never owned a radio but could tell stories until dawn, one who could spin and weave cloth but not figure out how to walk onto an escalator.

Once a man in a suit came to our fence to try to sell us insurance. Uncle Zovár did not understand why he should buy "e-chur-inz" if he was betting against his own good health. The man called my uncle an "ignorant oaf." But this salesman did not know my uncle, did not know that Uncle's life had been burnt to the ground and that he still remained kindly toward children, that he was still tender with animals, and that he still believed the land was a living being, one with its own hopes and needs and dreams.

LIKE THE OTHER REFUGEES IN OUR FAMILY, Uncle suffered from his memories, and he tried hard not to speak directly of his experiences in the war. But people have to speak of what has hurt them; otherwise the war beast jumps out in nightmares, sudden weeping, and fits of anger. When Uncle did speak of the past, his words were somehow far worse to hear when they were brief. He would say, "It was very bad." This was followed by a long silence.

More often he spoke in tales, and in the third person, such as, "I once knew 'this man' who said that the worst part of the slave camps was that loved ones were separated from one another. The mothers and fathers went insane, completely insane over the whereabouts of their sons and daughters. And the children, the children . . . "

And here Uncle would simply stop, rise up out of his chair, and walk outside. In rain, in snow, in daylight or night, he fled to the out-of-doors, and he would not return for a long time. I loved him and feared for him. During these times the adults suddenly and stonefacedly turned back to deliberately peeling their potatoes, knitting the socks, bringing in the wood, or sweeping the floor—all in utter silence, a silence that came from trying to protect themselves from their own loosely tethered ghosts.

But I ran out after Uncle and always found him walking down the road or, having stepped off the road into the fields, walking through the woods, or repairing little ropes and wires in the smokehouse. It was by running after Uncle that I came to learn about his odd friend and alter ego, "this man," . . . "the one that I once knew in the old country."

Uncle referred to "this man" so often over the years, that out of respect for the suffering that caused "this man" to come to life, I came to call this far-away spirit-self This Man, and sometimes, That Man, just like any personage worthy of a proper name.

Once Uncle told me, "This Man . . . This Man I used to know, he was haunted by the last images of the old women of the village as the wagon-trucks hauled the men and boys away. . . . They . . . the old women, with hardly any teeth left, howling, literally, to the heavens, lying down on the ground with the snow flying into their eyes and mouths, banging on the muddy ground, old women on their hands and knees, beating the ground with their fists in grief.

"This Man," my Uncle continued, "has so many memories. When the foreign army first came, and before they took everyone away, they said to This Man, 'If you just give us food, we will spare your grove of trees. Just tell us which stand of trees is yours, and we will spare it.'

"Trees, oh my God, the trees. We all grew stands of trees for love, for shade, for windbreaks. Sometimes, to see us through the winter, we sold some little part near the edge as a seedling crop when they were large enough.

"This Man had grown these trees, you see, grown them from their childhoods onward. They were his pride and joy.

"So, This Man tried to protect the trees. He, like all the rest of the farmers, had gone to the school of the fields, not the school of the teacher with eyeglasses. No one understood this war that swooped down like a giant hawk and carried entire villages off into the nest of hell, and no one knew how to escape.

"In desperation, This Man answered the soldiers, 'Which trees are mine? *All* the trees you see for as far as you can see, *all these* are my trees.' He pointed to not only his trees, but to those stands of all his neighbors, and to the ancient forest that stretched for miles beyond, all the way to the horizon.

"And for this answer they threw him to the ground, kicking him in the mouth over and over again for 'having a lying tongue.' They broke This Man's jaw, and they left him. In a rage they set fire to the immense deadwood at the centers of the biggest fir trees. The dry branches exploded in flames from the bottoms to the tops of the trees, and in so doing, burnt the stands of trees to the ground in a matter of moments."

FOR A LONG TIME OUR SMALL HOUSE WAS filled with many people who had just come from war—

and back from the dead. They carried hundreds of horrific images and losses that cannot be described in words alone.

Though my relatives gradually brought out their beautiful and haunting songs and their one-of-a-kind stories, the pain of war entrenched in mind and spirit went on, and on, and on. At first they could not cease speaking with great emotion about what had happened to them. Later, they made the most stalwart efforts never to speak about what had happened to them ever again. But, for a long time, the war beast had its way with them, in many ways and many times over.

What does it mean to live with a war and memories of war inside oneself? It means one lives in two worlds. One looking for hope, the other feeling hopeless. One looking for meaning, the other convinced that the only meaning in life is that there is no meaning in life.

In each of our people who had suffered so greatly, there were two struggling persons. One living the life of the new world, the other running, constantly running, from memories of hell that rose up and gave chase. Ghosts animated by themselves, roused by a click of a door frame, a cat in heat screeching suddenly in the night, the innocent dog at the screen door scratching to come in, a sudden gust of wind causing a curtain to sweep a jar off a table in a shot to the floor.

Mundane matters caused terror, tears, or revulsion: the smell of a certain gun oil, the first snow and fresh blood of deer gutted for food, a certain kind of bone ache from field work, an old story about a bridal veil, a sound of cattle hooves on a metal culvert, a sudden train whistle and the sound of the long trestle rumbling.

There were wars in Uncle that made him remember, as he said, "too much." There were wars between the death of hope, and the hope for death, the hope for life, and a life of hope. Sometimes the only cease-fire that held for any length of time had to be negotiated by a treaty forged with much schnapps and much vodka.

BUT THERE WERE ALSO TIMES OF GREAT PEACE, too. Uncle knew the land like he knew the lines on his face, like he knew the veins on the backs of his hands—the backyard, the side yard, and then out into the near field, and then the middle fields, and then the far fields. When we walked through these fields, our boots became heavier and heavier, clotted with black mud—one pound, then two pounds, then three pounds on each foot. The tops of our thigh muscles pulled hard. It took more and more tension to unstick one's last step in order to take the next. But this we loved—this small struggle that did no one harm. This was our modest proof that we were managing to live anew.

We walked, listening for the health of the plants and trees and crops about us. Was that bush filled with as many butterflies as needed? Were the trees filled with as many warbling birds as needed? Both birds and butterflies were critical, we knew, to the carrying of pollen among the fruit trees so there would be abundant cherry crops, so that there would be a goodly amount of pears and plums and peaches to be put up for winter.

As we walked, Uncle mused, "I have heard people ask, 'Where is the garden of Eden?' Ha! Anywhere we stand on this earth, we are standing right in the garden of Eden. This entire earth, underneath its rail tracks and highways, under its worn coat, under its rubble, under all these, is God's garden—still as fresh as the day it was created.

"It is true that in many places Eden is covered over and forgotten. But she can be made whole again. Wherever there is worn ground, misused or unused ground, Eden is still right beneath.

"But we would not gouge the earth back to life, nor try to bring Eden about in great shovelfuls. No, no. No matter how large the garden—one cubit by one, or huge fields you cannot see the end to—if you are directly planting, you do so by patting and patting the earth, taking little handfuls of it up. Be gentle, be economical. Do not take immense shovelfuls to get the job done faster. Like the pouring of milk into flour, you do not dump it all in at once. No, gently you pour a little, stir a little, pour a little more, stir a little more, and this is also how to treat the land, thoughtfully, with presence of mind."

This is how I learned that this land, which we depended upon for our food, our livelihoods, our rest, for

opportunity to meet beauty, ought to be treated in the
same manner that we would hope to treat others and
ourselves.Whatever happens to this field in some way
also happens to us.

All these matters we watched over so that we could
see the condition of everything, and how the crops would
be, and what was moving across the fields and in us.

We were content to live in these kinds of days, and
Uncle's wandering spirit, chased out of him by so much
war, began to hover near him again. And little by little
Uncle began to grow back into one person instead of two.

ALL WAS WELL AND GROWING GREEN AGAIN —
until there came a certain day. It began well enough in
the morning, but by early evening all hell had broken
loose.

The state road commission sent officials down to
announce to all in our rural village that the state would
"annex" land belonging to the people. The state would

build a toll-road through the quiet woodlands where we lived. They would "annex" entire forests and fields —these essentials that were the healing grounds of the war-torn, the land on which people grew their summer and winter food, the hide-and-seek places of children, the piney bedsteads of tramp rail-riders, the shelters of those who called a tarp and a stickpole home.

For ever so many, these lands were the rest and repair of our souls.

Uncle stood up and shouted, "What is *annex*? You mean *steal,* you *steal* from us!" Several frightened family members jostled Uncle out and tried to calm him.

The entire village reeled in dismay. The state condemned the land and the humble houses, the sagging barns, the tack and tool sheds so that the land could be bought for pennies on the dollar. Those who worked the land, those who loved the land, those who lived on and through the land, were allowed no recourse, no say-so.

For Uncle, and the other refugee-immigrants of our family and those of our many war survivor neighbors nearby, these events were terrifyingly close to the deep travails they had endured during the war: Their land was occupied against their wills; their farms, their crops, their livelihoods, and, more so, their spirits and what mattered to their spirits, were seized in an instant ... by men ... in uniforms ... who insisted ... who said they were only acting on orders ... who claimed their right over others ...

Uncle Zovár went temporarily mad.

THE FIRST DAY THE BULLDOZERS CAME, UNCLE railed and stomped through the fields, shaking his fist at the earthmovers far off in the distance. He tried to insult the drivers by yelling, *"Annyit ért hozzá, mint tyúk as ábécéhëz!"* The dozer operators, not understanding Hungarian, had no idea what he was saying. He was shouting, "You know as much about God's garden as a hen knows about the alphabet!"

In his misery and despair, Uncle scooped up a handful of little stones and with all his might threw them at the earthmoving machines. The pebbles hit the side of one of the machines with a sound like a handful of sand being thrown against an iron wall.

Two burly workmen escorted Uncle home, each holding him by one of his arms. Uncle was crying as they walked him to the house faster than he could keep up. "Keep this old man at home and out of our way," they snarled. They let go of Uncle's arms roughly, and he stumbled forward. My elderly aunt and I caught Uncle in our arms and brought him into the house. The big men swaggered back to their massive machines.

Uncle refused to be comforted. He called out, *"Kinyílik a bicska a zsebëmben!* My knife has opened in my pocket!" It was an old family way of saying one feels a terrible despair, and yet, is helpless to act. The relatives stood together in an anxious little huddle. They whispered, "Send in the child. . . . The child, the child. Send in the child . . ."

I went in to my uncle, and he tearfully took my hands. His words were ever so many, and I tried, but I could not quite grasp the meaning of his words with my mind. But the tone of his broken words and all the hopes and fears behind them, I felt these I not only understood, but that I could cry for him, and for all the people of the world, until the very end of time.

EVERYONE IN THE COMMUNITY PRAYED FOR THE road commission to come to their senses, for the bureaucrats to change their plans for the good of all, for the carving of the land to be stopped, for God to send this highway away, far away, forever.

But, it was not meant to be. Every day the earthmovers came, and every day they bleated and whined and ground, cutting down and through the prime forest and farmland.

ONE MORNING WE HEARD UNCLE OUTSIDE AND the sounds of hoes and rakes clashing and clattering and stacks of iron tools falling over. "I am doing something!" Uncle cried. "I am doing something!"

He seized two enormous shovels. Our shovels and hoes were sharpened on great whetstone wheels. All tool edges were sharp as razors. This was a holdover from the old country, where one might have to use one's tools not only to dig, but also to defend oneself. No one had lived long enough away from war to have found reason to outgrow this practice.

Everyone cried, "No, Zovár! No! Put the shovels down! What are you doing?! Do not do something rash! Zovár! Zováááárrr!"

But Uncle did not answer. He marched toward the fields with a shovel on either shoulder, "one to rest, one to work." All morning he dug in a small parcel of what was left of a larger field after the toll-road bed cut through. In their passion to make the road, some workers had plowed up more field-land than needed. The broken trunks of trees and the destroyed corn rows were all they had left behind. They'd turned a living field into debris and then walked away. The new toll-road was now complete, and its pavement lay less than three hundred yards to the west.

Uncle dug deeply along the perimeter of the field following the general camber of the new highway, and leaving behind a long snaking mound of dirt. He dug and shoveled and shoveled and dug. Various neighbor men interrupted their own work to walk down the road to advise. They returned with shovels and pick-axes to help.

By afternoon, for as far as one could see, there was a trench that ran along the edge of about one-half of one hectare. It was perhaps two cubits wide along the narrow side of the field that would remain in village hands.[7]

Night fell. Uncle trudged home. He ate a big meal of soup from a pottery bowl with a Magyar bird painted on its side. He chewed down a chunk of black home-made rye bread. He downed stinging cold beer from an amber glass bottle.

He left the house carrying an old dented red bucket brimming with fuel. He walked, tilted way over to one side with his burden.

There in the field, in the completely windless night, he carefully poured the fuel all along the field on two sides and once down the middle. From the edge of the field, he struck wooden stick matches and threw them in low at several places.

The entire field erupted in a blaze so great that it drew people from as far away as the black smoke cloud could be seen.

The wide dirt roads on three sides and the trench on one side kept the blaze contained.

Far into the night, men and women with sleepy children in their arms stood in long orange lines, nodding their heads approvingly, and watching the field burn and burn.

THE NEXT DAY, THE FIELD WAS STILL SMOKING but fire-dead. With his razor-sharp hoe, Uncle skinned back blackened roots and stubble here and there, thereby exposing the earth even more.

"So you see," Uncle said, "this burning and black-ening of the soil here? Soon much will come of it, so much that you will not believe it."

"What will you seed here?" I asked.

"I will seed nothing," said Uncle.

I did not understand. We had burnt land before, for the ash made tired ground more fertile again.

"Why will you leave the land bare and unseeded, Uncle?"

"Ah, as an invitation, my girl."

Uncle explained that the pines and oaks will not spread into the fields to grow and make a new woods, unless we leave the ground unseeded. My uncle envi-sioned that this barren land was to become a new forest, one of great beauty and repose. "To be poor and be without trees, is to be the most starved human being in the world. To be poor and to have trees, is to be com-pletely rich in ways that money can never buy."

The trees, he said, would not come if the land were planted. "The seeds of new life will find no hospitality or reason to rest here unless we leave it barren, unless we leave it bare so that a forest of seeds will find it hospitable."

Long ago Uncle's father had a good friend who gave him these words, and these my uncle taught to me: *hachmasat orchim.* They mean hospitality, especially to strangers. Uncle explained that this was the principle by which they strove to live before the war, the principle by which they attempted to live during the war, and now again after the war, it was the principle we were to use in order to try to live again.[8]

Uncle said that it was a blessing to welcome the stranger, to give comfort to the wanderer, and especially to the weary traveler. "Just as the hospitable laugh waits for a joke it can laugh at, just as the dying are hospitable in awaiting with grace the arrival of The One, so, too, the land has the hospitality of a true host.

"For the earth is so patient. See? It takes the seed, the weed, the tree, the flower; it takes the rain, the grain, the fire. It allows and invites entry. It is the perfect host," said Uncle.

I understood. The seeds of the earth, the creatures

of the earth, the stars overhead, and we ourselves—we were all the guests of this field.

So we left the land bare, so that the seeds would know to find their way to it. They would be carried in the mouths of small animals who might know this field was waiting. They would drop the seeds here. The raccoon would eat and deposit what was left in the field. The deer scratching against a post would release the seeds riding in its pelt, the mourning doves flying over might drop seeds from their beaks, the weather in the sky and the air would join together to bring in seeds on the wind as well.

"You will see, all because of the tremendous *hachmasat orchim* of this land, a great thing will begin to happen here.

"Do you know how to make trees grow, as wild and beautiful as any you have ever seen? You leave the land hospitable. How do you do that?

"It is not a surprise. As for a guest, first you put out water. Oh, God has already done this for us. Here in the fields, God calls this rain. What a great host is God!

"Well, next you put out sun and some shade. Oh, in the clouds and sun, God has taken care of this also. Oh, what a great host is God!

"Lastly, you leave the ground fallow. What does that mean? It means you leave it turned, but unsown. It means you send it through fire in order to prepare it for its new life.

"This is the part God does not do alone. God likes a partnership. It is up to us to help what God has begun. No one wants this kind of burning, this kind of fire. We want the field to remain as it once was, in its pristine beauty, just as we want life to remain as it once was.

"But fire comes. Though we are afraid, it comes anyway, sometimes by accident, sometimes on purpose, sometimes for reasons no one can understand—reasons that are God's business alone.

"But the fire can also turn everything to a new direction, a new and different life, one that has its own strengths and ways to shape the world."

I could already see that this was in somewise true. I could see with my own eyes that just overnight the field was already alive again with the tiniest life—

walking-stick creatures that stood out like bright green straws against the black ash at the edge of the field, and ant men in black trousers and red waistcoats were strolling about here and there.

"There is a story I will tell you," said Uncle, "a story about the time of peace and the time of ashes, about how the young and the old learn about that which can never die."

Uncle pulled a big untidy cigar from the cotton bag he wore around his waist when he was in the fields. Among other items in this bag were his knife, a spare neckerchief, a few iron nails for the fruit trees,[9] stick matches, and a little, long-haired goatskin flask of "liquid remedy." Uncle had told me before, "This is a remedy, for if I cut myself, I can pour it on the cut. If I am lucky enough not to cut myself, then I drink this remedy every day in order to stay healthy."

He bit off the end of the cigar and trimmed it with his knife. He puffed and puffed to light it. He stuck his knife in the ground to one side. We sat down there at the edge of the small blackened field surrounded by taller fields filled with ripening corn. Uncle's long pleated pantaloons flowed around his boots. His big hat shaded his face. I sat with my legs straight out, the toes of my scuffed brown shoes turned inward, the shoes' old straps curled at the ends just after they passed through the rusty buckles.

"You see," said Uncle, "once upon a time, a long, long time ago, during the time that the blessed animals could still speak . . .

That Which Can Never Die

. . . and humans could still understand the language of animals, there was a young fir tree who, though small in stature, was vast in spirit.

He lived deep in a forest surrounded by trees far greater, far more majestic, and far more ancient than any heretofore known.

Each winter, fathers and mothers and their children traveled deep into the forest in old wooden sleighs. With much happiness and festivity they cut several of the medium-sized trees and carried them off. The venerable horses drawing the sleighs snuffled, and the bells on their harnesses went ring-ting-a-ling. The laughter of the children and the grown-ups rang out all through the woods.

Oh, yes, the little fir tree had heard it whispered about among the oldest trees, those who were too tall and too great to be taken by the axe and hauled away—oh yes, he had heard that the trees that were cut down were taken to a wondrous place, to something called a home.

There they were treated with greatest respect, smoothed by many hands, and placed in a soothing water. Then, it was said, an entire family of smiling people gathered around. They dressed the tree with small, beautiful objects: little globes made of ribbon with nut-meats inside, and sugar cookies and other goodies. Glorious little candles were lit and placed in the crooks and arms of the tree. So finally, there festooned with candies, strings of fruit, and sometimes even glass ornaments and tiny colored mirrors, the tree became the most honored guest of the home. It was indeed one of the most magnificent glories that any tree could ever be granted.

Amongst the oldest trees who knew about these matters, it was said that this was, for the humans concerned, a time of great joy, for beautiful little children came singing, and the fires burned in every hearth, and even the stars of the sky seemed to shine all the more.

As the old ones described it, hither and yon young women and young men could be found scurrying and carrying into the parlor whatever food they had to share with all. The old women were in their best white aprons. The old men wore their best black suits and black hats, and all the women wore their best black dresses. All the boys were in trousers that always itched, and girls were in skirts just right for practicing curtsies. Oh, it all sounded completely wonderful. And this is what the fir tree dreamed about.

Year after year the fir tree waited for summer to pass, for autumn to arrive, and finally for the lovely winter to come. When he felt the bite of the chill winds, he rejoiced. He was most happy then in his great green coat that grew fuller with each passing year. And every year, too, in the winter, the sleighs came and cut the trees again, while the children shouted and made snow angels in the great drifts.

And though the little fir tree was shy, he could not help himself and cried out more boldly each year, "Come! Choose me! Choose me! I *love* children. I *love* this fabled celebration that you do. Choose me! Please! Choose me!"

But year after year, no one chose him. Soon many trees had been taken from the forest around him. Now his nearest relative stood quite far off, and the little fir tree stood rather alone, but also, in full sunshine, and so he grew, and grew, and *grew* much taller than ever before.

In the following winter, again came horses pulling a sleigh of laughing children, mother, and father. The horses pranced right past the fir tree, for the father was assessing the thick groves of trees far ahead. "Wait," cried one of the children, "that one back there, that one standing all by itself." And the fir tree began to tremble with hope.

"Oh yes! Come closer! Choose me! Please! Choose me!" The fir tree struggled to stand straighter and taller. And the family must have heard him, for the sleigh stopped, and the horses trotted around about and made their way back, and soon the family was pushing their way through the deep snow to inspect the tree.

"Oh, see how bouncy are its branches," cried one child who had the most perfect ruddy cheeks. "Oh, see how green and fresh this tree is," said the mother. "Yes," said the father, "this one looks not too tall and not too short, but rather, just right for us."

And the father brought his axe from the sleigh. At its first strike, the fir tree felt the greatest pain he had ever known in his entire life. "Oh," cried the tree, "I fall." And right there and then, he swooned. The axe continued to strike until the tree was severed from its root, falling over in a great shower of snow.

Much later, the fir tree came to on the sled swaying behind the sleigh. The bells on the harnesses of the horses tinkled, and the fir tree could hear people talking and laughing. The most terrible of the pain seemed to be passing now, and besides, he remembered vaguely, they were going somewhere, somewhere important, somewhere beautiful and wondrous, some-where he had wished and wished to see all the days and years of his life past.

Here, Uncle paused to trim his shaggy cigar. "You know, my girl, do you not, what we say at times like this in such a story?" I did know, for we had played this game many times before.[10]

"Yes," I piped up. "At the first turn in the story, we say at moments like these, 'Like gypsies, when the caravan begins to sway forward, even though one is leaving one place known, for another place unknown, no one is ever sad.'"

"Very good," smiled Uncle, and ruffled my hair. "For that fine reply you shall be rewarded with the next part of the story."

At last, as darkness fell, the sleigh with the family in it and the tree on the sled behind it, came to a halt before a snow-covered cottage. An old man and old woman came out into the snow and gathered around the sled exclaiming, "What a fine, fine tree, so tall and so wide. Just the right size. Just perfect."

"Oh," thought the fir tree, "how good it is to be welcomed. I wonder if this is the place where some of my kin have come to over all these years. Oh, I hope I shall see them again soon."

The old people lifted him down from the sled with gentle hands. They admired him, patted him, turning him this way and that. They placed the cut trunk of the tree into a bucket of cool water that soothed much of his soreness.

And as they turned out the lanterns, the fir tree who loved the deep and dark of the forest, began also to love the darkness of this home. Even though he was used to seeing the entire night sky of stars, and now could see only a bit of night sky through a small pane of window, there was one star that twinkled more than the others. And seeing this, the fir tree felt there was much promise yet to come.

With these thoughts, he, like the rest of the household, soon fell happily and fast asleep.

Early the next morning, there was much noise and commotion with everyone greeting, complaining, and gossiping. Someone was knocking the dust out of the wood-chip bucket and filling it—clank, clunk, clunk. The dogs raced in yip, yip, yipping, followed by the children, and then the mother and father, and then the old ones, and other children and friends as well, all carrying many boxes.

The tree waited, veritably holding its breath with excitement. The people pulled the covers off the boxes, and inside were ornaments of all shapes and sizes, made of the thinnest glass. There were strings of cranberries, and candles with little colored papers set into glass cups.

Around and around, the tree was strung and draped with these. And then, oh glory be, dozens of candles were lit, one after the other, and these were placed in circles and spirals higher and higher in his boughs, and the fir tree was in his absolute glory.

"Oh, this is all that the old ones back in the forest described, and so much more," exclaimed the fir tree. And he made a great effort to stretch out his limbs farther, and he tried to look as handsome as possible. The children cried out and ran in circles around him, while others played music and sang, and oh, what joy, especially when one beautiful child, held up by his grandfather, placed a paper star upon the crown branch at the very top of the tree.

That night, after the children were asleep and the fir tree was drowsing, and as that great star shone through the windows, the old ones crept into the room with gifts wrapped with beautiful soft brown paper and in cloth scraps that they had pieced together with bright embroidery floss. They placed on the mantle little horses, pigs and ducks, and cows made from apples and oranges with twigs stuck into them for legs, and eyes and noses carved onto them to make them smile. And all of these were made with hands filled with the kind of love that desires to surprise and delight little children.

In the morning the tree awakened with a start as the children came racing in shrieking and exclaiming, "Oh, look at the beautiful tree and the gifts beneath." And they pulled open the wrappings and held up lovely rag dolls with rich brown yarn curls and hand-crocheted dresses. Next they unwrapped wagons made from scrap wood with wheels that really turned.

They happily tore the nutmeats from the fir tree, and the tree rustled its branches in happiness to be so much a part of all that he had dreamed, and more.

By late in the day, the children were napping on the rug and the grown-ups snoozed as well, and even the dogs and the cats were asleep and dreaming. And the tree reflected on its exquisite fate and all the events that had come to pass. And he was very, very happy.

That night as all were abed and snoring softly—the dog and cat like this: zzzzzz, and the children like this: zzzzzz, and the mother and father and old ones like this: ZZZZZZ—

the tree slept deeply also and dreamed of his new life.

The following day and the next, the tree stood proudly in the room, even though a bit bedraggled from having all its ribbons torn from it and its star tipped over one of its eyes. Nevertheless, all was glorious even as the fir tree saw most of the children and grown-ups climb into their sleighs and depart. "Oh, they will be back tonight," thought the fir tree, "and then they will put my sore trunk in fresh and cool water once again. They will decorate me once more, and the celebration will begin all over again."

The father tramped in then and stripped the ornaments from the fir tree, laying these in boxes in layers of cotton batting. Then, he pulled the tree from its water, and shook it so hard that whatever else might have been hidden in its boughs fell to the floor. He left the strands of dried cranberries on the tree and dragged it from the room.

The fir tree, though startled at this brusque treatment, was yet hopeful. "Oh, I wonder what room we are going to next." He imagined the entire joyous process of decorating and gifts and children dancing and everyone singing, and he sighed to think of it all.

But, the father hauled the fir tree roughly up the wooden staircase that led upward and upward, the steps becoming more and more narrow the higher they climbed. And at last, at the topmost landing, the father opened a small door and, without ceremony, threw the tree inside. The tree cried out in alarm in what seemed to him like a great shout, "What darkness is this?" But, in fact, no one seemed to hear, for the father shut the door and retreated down the stairs.

Here Uncle sighed, the stub of his cigar held in those startling dark teeth of his. "Ah," he said, "here we are at the place in the story of this little life, where the only change that is certain is that there will be change. Do you understand what I say?"

I thought I understood, but I was not sure. I thought for a good, long while. Ought I reply, "If the violin player has lost his violin, he can still sing"?

No. I could see from Uncle's solemn face that this was not the right answer.

Was it, "In the army there is no *Péter bátya?* In the army there is no Uncle Peter?" this meaning that, under extreme duress, there is no nice overseer to bind up one's wounds.[11]

No, I could see that that was not the right answer either.

Uncle's face was completely attentive. He was waiting, like a dog waits, with the slightest trembling just under the skin. Uncle was waiting for me to say just one right word, and if or when I did, he would be ready to instantly nod or wink, to smile or shout or slap his knee.

Then I remembered. I tried it out, lowering my voice. "Does it mean, dear Uncle, that though we think we are following the rightful map . . . "

Uncle began to smile.

". . . that God suddenly decides to lift up the road
. . ."

Uncle began to nod happily.

"And places it and us elsewhere?"

"Oh, school is not wasted on you, my child," Uncle roared.[12] "Yes, though we think we are following the rightful map, God suddenly decides to lift up the road, placing it and us elsewhere! That is it *exactly!*"

He placed his big hands on each side of my face. "*Now* you have earned the rest of the story."

. . . So, you see, in this small, cold attic room, there was no light save for one small frosty window in the eaves of the house, through which shone that great star.

"Oh, woe is me," thought the tree, feeling all its limbs to see if anything was broken. "What have I done that I should be abandoned in such a cold and lonely place?"

But no one heard. And there the fir tree remained for many days and nights.

One particular night, however, out of the corner of its eye, the tree saw four glowing red dots, and these were the eyes of two tiny mice who occupied the attic walls. "Oh," he said to them softly, "oh, my ladies, do you know when they will come to take me from this attic and carry me to the special room again?" The mouse in the coveralls and muffler began to chatter and laugh, "C-c-c-come to get you and take you to the special r-room again? Ha ha ha."

But the other mouse in her little gown and white apron elbowed her friend and spoke to the tree in a kindly way: "Oh, dear tree, why, you have just lived a good life, have you not?"

"Yes," nodded the tree sadly.

"Ah, I know that you felt born to this life —so much so that you did not wish for it to change. But . . . ," and here she patted the tree, "all things, dear tree, even good things, come to an end."

"This time must end?" the fir tree cried.

"Yes," said the little mouse, reaching up and patting the tree again. "Yes, this time has come to an end. But now a different time begins. A new life, a different kind of life always follows the old. You'll see."

And the two little mice sat with the tree throughout the night, and they told stories and sang all the songs they knew. And the fir tree asked if the mice would like to climb into its boughs to stay warmer, and they said thank you very much they would, and they did so. And together they all slept through the dark night with the great star outside the window coming closer and closer, almost as though it knew their truth and, taking pity, shone its light ever more deeply upon them.

In the morning the fir tree and the mice were rudely awakened by the sound of heavy footfalls on the stairs, and the mouse couple jumped from the limbs of the fir tree. "Farewell, dear friend. Remember us as we shall remember you and your kindness." And the mice ran for the crevice in the wall.

"And I, you," called the tree. "And I shall remember you."

The attic door banged open, and the father, wearing a woolen cap and greatcoat, seized the fir tree and dragged it down the many stairs, through the door, and out into the yard. There he laid the fir tree across an old stump and hoisted high a great axe, which fell upon the tree with the most terrible weight, causing the most awful sounds of tearing wood. At the first chop, the tree thought it would die from the pain, and by the second, it had fainted dead away.

A long while later, the fir tree awakened in the corner of the special room again and, while not quite itself, seemed to be missing only its greenery, and its arms were arranged quite differently and rather in pieces. But he saw there, in the chairs before the fireplace, the old couple who had first cared for him when he came to their home from the forest. They were the ones who long ago had soothed his wound with cool water. There they were, drawn close together before the fire. In spite of his condition, the fir tree smiled at the love he saw between them.

The old man rose and put one of the arms of the fir tree into the fire, and though at first the fir tree resisted and cried out, he soon understood, as the flame burned more and more deeply into the heart of himself, that this was his joyous work in the world—to create a warmth for such as these. Oh, to be warmed from the inside by love, and from the outside by the love of one such as he.

The fir tree burnt ever harder and stronger then. "Oh, I never knew I could burn with such brightness, that I could fill a room with such warmth. I love these old ones with all my heart." The fir tree and all the knots in its wood—and in its heart—burst with joy in the flame.[13]

Night after night, the fir tree surrendered himself to this rendering. He was so completely glad to be useful and to be alive in this way, that he burned and burned until there was no more left of him, except for the ashes that lay in the bottom of the grate.

And as he was being brushed out of the grate by the old people, he thought he had never imagined more glory than his life had been till now, and that he could never again wish for more than had been his life up to this very moment.

The elderly couple was very careful, and with their wise old hands they gently swept out every bit of ash from the fire pit. They placed the ashes in a soft and well-used bag. And this they stored away until the springtime arrived.

At the first warming of the earth, the old man and old woman brought out the bag of ashes, entered their gardens and fields, and carefully spread the ashes of the fir tree throughout and over all their fruiting vines, over all their land as well. They mixed the fir tree's ashes in with the soil. Over time, as the springtime rains and sun came and stayed, the ashes of the fir tree felt a quickening beneath himself.

Here and there, all below and through and around the ashes, came tiny bright green shoots breaking through the ground, and the fir tree smiled a thousand smiles and sighed a thousand sighs in its happiness for being useful once again.

"Oh, I never knew one could fall to such ashes and yet bring forth such new life again. What great luck has come into my life. I grew up in the solitude of the forest. Later, what fine days and nights of tinkling glasses and candlelight and singing I did come to know. In my time of loneliness and need in the darkest night, I was befriended by strangers, those who wanted to be family, and more. Even as I was being rendered by the fire, I found I could give forth immense light and warmth from the heart of me. What luck, what fortune I have had.

"Ah," sighed the fir tree, "of all that rises and falls and rises again, it is love of new life, and love of that alone, that lasts and lasts. I am everywhere now. See how far my reach?"

And that night, as the great star traversed the universe's night sky, the fir tree lay in the blessed earth, hovering close to all the roots and seeds to warm them, his own ashes nourishing forever all things that grow, and these in turn nourishing others, who in turn would nourish others yet, and for all generations to come. In that beauteous earth, from whence he came and now to which he was returned, he slept well and dreamed deeply, surrounded there—as he had been once before in the deep forest—by that which is far greater, far more majestic, and far more ancient than any heretofore known.

"Do you see, my child? *Nincs oly hitrány eszköz, hogy hasznát në lёhetne vënni.* There is no worthless thing. Everything can be used for something. In God's garden, there is a usefulness for everyone and everything."

In our family we say, "Go out into the fields to weep, for there your tears will do both you and the land great good." Uncle and I sat in the field for a good long while, alternately talking softly, trading stories, and weeping just a little at the sad and happy parts of our lives and of the tales. Finally, Uncle said, "I pronounce that we have properly christened this ground completely." He dried his eyes with the backs of his big hands. He put his arm around me and brushed my tears away with the long ends of his neckerchief.

It was late and time for us to be going home. Uncle pulled me to my feet, and we hoisted the hoes onto our shoulders, he helping me to find just the right balance for the hoe's weight.

"Let us see," he said as we walked, "what will become of our field. Perhaps by morning it will be an entire forest again." He laughed and bent down to straighten my hoe, giving me a great big wink.

We walked home through the dusk, the burnt ground sleeping for now in the twilight behind us.

And, as we slept that night, seeds from all corners of our world began to travel toward the open field with all Godspeed.

AND SO IT CAME TO BE THAT OVER TIME THIS FIELD, opened by burning—this field, fallow and waiting—drew just the right strangers, just the right seeds to itself. In all due time, tiny trees began to appear. The oaks came, the white pines came, the silver and red maples came, and even green and red willows found their way to the farthest bend of the hospitable field where there was a small groundwater waiting for them. To Uncle, these trees were like young people, alive and courting and dancing again. He was ever so joyous, and so was I.

Over a long period of time—for hardwood trees grow slowly—there grew up a small forest and a thick ground cover, with plenty of thatch for snow forts and secret places for sheltering children at their games, and small dappled clearings that made praying and resting places for many kinds of wanderers and travelers. This forest became a living home for the orange and black orioles, the scarlet cardinals, and blue, blue, blue-jays; these we called "God's forest jewels." Here, too, there came butterflies landing with the tiniest thuds on the slender grasses, making the long blades sway just the littlest bit from their delicate weights.

Also, in the early morning, for just a very few minutes, if you rose early enough, you could see the dew outlining every shape in the forest for as far as you could see. Like tiny strings of lights, the dew edged every thorn, every bristle, every serrated edge of every long grass, every point of every single leaf. It clung to every rough edge of tree bark, to every stick, to every forgotten child's toy left in the woods. In early light, the once empty field, now forest, shone like a palace where every shape took light, and returned it to us a thousandfold. Uncle and I felt certain we stood in God's great garden, Eden.

FORTY-FIVE YEARS PASSED THROUGH US. Uncle stayed alive for many years, his long life attributable, I believe, to this immutable and faithful force that moves all human beings toward new life no matter what fire has taken them down.

Over the years, along with all the actual fields he helped to sow, fallow fields were resown inside him. His life force gathered momentum and broke through the ground again. He grew up through the ashes, through the empty field of himself. I witnessed in him a small parcel of Eden restored. I know it is so. I saw it with my own eyes.

When at last he prepared to leave this world, he crashed down like one of the old tall trees. And like a great tree fallen, but not severed from its roots, he lingered for several more seasons, leafing out again here and there, over a period of time, and bravely. Then one night, in a wind of the proper kind, the last bands of his old wood split apart, and he was free at last.

I grieved then, and grieve still, for not just one passing soul, but for two: for the old, old man who was my dearest Uncle. And for the beloved and ever-loyal This Man.

THE LESSONS OF UNCLE, THE LESSONS OF THE groves of trees in the old country, the lessons of the fallow field, the lessons of our stories that were shaped by war and starvation and hope—all these remain brilliantly alive in spirit, and in me, and, through me, in my children, and in my children's children, and I hope, in their children as well.

I feel that Zovár's spirit lives on. He and This Man's many stories of the old country—and the new country —live on through every empty field, through any and all who take the role of the host, waiting patiently, faithfully for the new seed to arrive and grow a bounty there, as indeed it will. I am certain that in every fallow place, new life is waiting to be born anew. And more astonishing yet, that new life will come whether one wills it or not. One may try to uproot it each time, but each time it will re-root and re-found itself again. New seed will fly in on the wind, and it will keep arriving, giving many chances for change of heart, return of heart, mending of heart, and for choosing life again at long last—of all this I am certain.

What is that which can never die? It is that faithful force that is born into us, that one that is greater than us, that calls new seed to the open and battered and barren

places, so that we can be resown. It is this force, in its
insistence, in its loyalty to us, in its love of us,
in its most often mysterious ways, that is
far greater, far more majestic,
and far more ancient
than any heretofore
ever known.

Epilogue

AS I COMPLETE THIS BOOK, I LOOK OUT INTO the little tree farm I began to grow three years ago when I first began to write *The Faithful Gardener.* I began the tree farm and the book as active prayers in honor of Uncle and my other refugee dear ones, and to entreat the strongest intercession and blessing I know to be shed down on those millions in the world who, of necessity, often not of their choice or of their making, struggle to walk an unfamiliar or painful road.

To create this living prayer, I began by digging out a wide swath of turf and making certain ablutions over the soil, as is our custom. Then I set the small parcel of ground afire—a low fire trenched on all sides on a completely windless day.[14] Afterward, I left the ground fallow.

The first year and following, a sufficient amount of tears were cried into the soil so that the ground could be proclaimed properly christened.

Then, I waited and waited, watching over this empty little plot. In the midst of our brick-bungalow village, would any seed be able to find its way to this tiny empty field?

Neighbors and passers-by stopped to ask why the yard was "torn up." "Why is it so naked?" Didn't I plan to put down some nice Kentucky Blue? "You gonna build a big garage?" I stood by my homely fallow land.

"You're growing a *what?*"

"I am growing a forest in the city, an urban forest."

People went away scratching their heads.

A village inspector stopped by. He said he had heard that someone in the neighborhood was building a forest in their backyard.

"Doesn't look like a forest," he said.

"Wait," I said.

"Might be illegal," he said.

"As you can see, at this point it is only a forest in the air."[15]

"Hmmf," he said.

THE SECOND YEAR, THERE CAME THE FAITHFUL miracle. Tiny trees began to appear in the fallow ground, trees so small that one would be tempted to tell children that these were lived in by elves. There were the tiniest sprig of spruce, a delicate red-stemmed maple, and seven baby bays from a huge mother tree down the road.

At the end of the third year now, there are two maples four feet tall, fifteen bays, two ash trees almost five feet tall, three golden rain trees whose small puffed-up lanterns have bloomed twice, and twenty-seven elm starts.

As amazing, it appears as though the earth remembers its own most ancient patterns, for beneath the saplings, little grape ivies and fernleaf and other ground covers have begun to grow. Full-headed clover has broken through the skin of this earth. Flickers, sparrows and woodpeckers, and other small animals have brought seeds of various sorts. There is the start of a wild strawberry vine, and there are wild onions. There is *yerba buena,* there is mint, there is *yanica,* and other herbs, all thriving as though nature has a tremendous love for the medicinal as well as for the beauteous.

Onto this plot of land that once held so little, also have come new butterflies, the flying red-spotted ladies, and crickets—not the usual tired-out urban crickets who say "twe-twe," but crickets that sing four-part harmonies and ring like bells, "twetwetwetwetwetwe. . . ." There is an old wooden garden wall that protects the little tree farm from north winds in winter. The stars overhead can now shine down on another tiny part of reclaimed Eden.

This miracle of new life made in fallow ground is an old, old story. In ancient Greece, Persephone, the maiden Goddess of the earth, was captured and held for a long time underground. During that time, her mother, the earth itself, so missed her lovely spirit that she became barren, and a cold and sterile Ever-winter fell across the land.

When Persephone was finally released from the travails of hell, she returned to the earth with such joy, that every step of her bare foot that touched the barren ground instantly caused a swath of green and flowers to spread in every direction.

THROUGH THIS LITTLE URBAN FOREST I CONTEMPLATE my refugee foster family, the faithful ones who, long ago, through fate, became my own. How a child torn in one way came together with those torn in another way is a destiny that seems, as we say, "God's plan and God's business."

I understand less of what I gave to my foster family and much more of what they gave to me. Love, oh yes, wisdom, oh yes, and sustained harshnesses of certain kinds that abraded the rough edges of something hopefully valuable and worthy of being polished in me. They offered hard trials of many kinds, and a pure respect for survival—not of the fittest—but of the wisest, of those most devoted to life, to the land, to one's loved ones, including those who are hard to love, and to those who need love more than anything.

Through the lives we lived, I learned the harshest gift-lesson to accept, and the most powerful I know— that is, *knowledge,* an absolute certainty that life repeats itself, renews itself, no matter how many times it is stabbed, stripped to the bone, hurled to the ground, hurt, ridiculed, ignored, scorned, looked down upon, tortured, or made helpless.[16]

I learned from my dear people as much about the grave, about facing the demons, and about rebirth as I have learned in all my psychoanalytic training and all my twenty-five years of clinical practice. I know that those who are in some ways and for some time shorn of belief in life itself—that they ultimately are the ones who will come to know best that Eden lies underneath the empty field, that the new seed goes first to the empty and open places—even when the open place is a grieving heart, a tortured mind, or a devasted spirit.

What is this faithful process of spirit and seed that touches empty ground and makes it rich again? Its greater workings I cannot claim to understand. But I know this: Whatever we set our days to might be the least of what we do, if we do not also understand that something is waiting for us to make ground for it, something that lingers near us, something that loves, something that waits for the right ground to be made so it can make its full presence known.

I am certain that as we stand in the care of this faithful force, that what has seemed dead is dead no longer, what has seemed lost, is no longer lost, that which some have claimed impossible, is made clearly possible, and what ground is fallow is only resting— resting and waiting for the blessed seed to arrive on the wind with all Godspeed.[17]

And it will.

A Prayer

Refuse to fall down.
If you cannot refuse to fall down,
refuse to stay down.
If you cannot refuse to stay down,
lift your heart toward heaven,
and like a hungry beggar,
ask that it be filled,
and it will be filled.
You may be pushed down.
You may be kept from rising.
But no one can keep you
from lifting your heart
toward heaven—
only you.
It is in the middle of misery
that so much becomes clear.
The one who says nothing good
came of this,
is not yet listening.

C. P. ESTÉS

Notes

1. In the old country, there are certain stories that, like friends, "go with one another" for various sensible and spiritual reasons. In my family, the knowledge of these combinations and their artful structures and subtexts is learned from decades of apprenticeship, that is, listening with outer and inner hearing to the elders, who listened in these ways to their elders, who likewise critically listened to their elders, and so on.

2. My earliest stories grew, in part, from trading endless parables with my Aunt Káti, one of my father's elderly sisters and one of my great mentors. In particular, she kept the ritual of telling the old country Bible stories on specific Holy Days, Name Days, Feast Days, and Days of Obligation.

3. This story is excerpted from a longer literary story created by the author, "The Creation of Stories," copyright © 1970, C. P. Estés.

4. A play on *szivar*, which means "cigar."

5. When a war is "over," it is never simply "over." The first war takes place during wartime. The second war, the far longer one, occurs when the fighting stops; this war is not over for years, most often for generations to come.

6. These handmade shoes are called *bocskorok*. The thin, tanned hide soles are whipstitched to knitted uppers, "so you can feel the ground you walk upon." That a single *bocskorok* could fit on either foot was an endless fascination to me as a child.

7. A hectare is about two and a half acres; a cubit, about twenty inches.

8. Many in our family felt that in every Christian were still the roots of the first-century or further-back ancient Jewish faith. In our old-country roots we have many concepts that are Hebraic in nature, for instance the concept of *mitzvah*, the blessing, and in particular, the *mitzvah* of the bringing of guests into one's living space.

9. In our time it was understood that piercing the bark of a waning fruit tree with iron nails would often bring it to new life again. The symbolism of living wood pierced by nails was not lost on us.

10. One of the ways in which I was apprenticed to the healing nature of stories was by practicing call and response as led by my elders. There are certain wisdoms that are to be understood in specific stories. Though some might think this particular way of teaching quaint, it is quite a sophisticated and complex form of handing down insights about life, via an exegesis of the subtext of particular stories.

11. *Nincs a hadban sémmi Péter bátya.* In the army there is no Uncle Peter.

12. Many in my family felt that it was a waste of time to educate girls. One of my grandmothers, however, even though she herself could neither read nor write, used to rail about this, saying that to educate a woman was to educate her whole family.

13. In a quite different and much shorter story, Hans Christian Andersen ends with a tree burning in the fire, and that is that. The stories that derive from the humus of our family are peculiar in that many are darker and carry one-of-a-kind "completions" in ways that the cleaned-up and prettified "classics" most often do not. To my mind, it is our eye-witness and face-to-face encounters with death, first-hand encounters with the terrors of humanity, that cause my family stories to retain their redemptive shapes.

14. If you have never set a ground fire, you absolutely ought not to, period.

15. In all levity, perhaps we ought to apply to the federal government for a "tiniest national forest" designation.

16. From the dozens of refugee family members who raised me, I learned, from the utter inside out, about soul and psyche—its woundings, its mournings, and its ultimate mending. As the only living child of the family at that time, I learned about not only the darker and more resilient aspects of life, but also about the constant proximity of death, in ways and in depths normally reserved to the very old.

17. This wind from ancient times that Uncle spoke about is called *Ruach.* He explained to me that *Ruach* is the Hebraic wind of wisdom, the wind that unites humans and God. *Ruach* is the breath of God that reaches down to earth in order to awaken and reawaken souls.

Resources

Audio

Clarissa Pinkola Estés, Ph.D., is the creator of a collection of original audio works combining myths and stories with archetypal analysis and psychological commentary. Titles include:

The Faithful Gardener:
A Wise Tale About That Which Can Never Die
(90 minutes)

Women Who Run with the Wolves:
Myths and Stories on the Instinctual Nature of Women
(180 minutes)

The Creative Fire:
Myths and Stories on the Cycles of Creativity
(180 minutes)

Theatre of the Imagination:
A twelve-part series of myths, stories, and commentaries broadcast over National Public Radio and Pacifica Networks nationwide
(1080 minutes)

Warming the Stone Child:
Myths and Stories About Abandonment and the Unmothered Child
(90 minutes)

The Radiant Coat:
Myths and Stories on the Crossing Between Life and Death
(90 minutes)

In the House of the Riddle Mother:
Archetypal Motifs in Women's Dreams
(180 minutes)

The Red Shoes: On Torment and the Recovery of Soul Life
(80 minutes)

The Gift of Story: A Wise Tale About What Is Enough
(60 minutes)

The Boy Who Married an Eagle:
Myths and Stories on Male Individuation
(90 minutes)

How to Love a Woman:
On Intimacy and the Erotic Life of Women
(180 minutes)

For information about these and other new audio releases by Dr. Estés,
write or call Sounds True, 735 Walnut St., Dept. FGX, Boulder, CO
80302. Phone 1-800-333-9185.

Books

Women Who Run with the Wolves: Myths and Stories of the
Wild Woman Archetype. New York: Ballantine, 1992

The Gift of Story: A Wise Tale About What Is Enough.
New York: Ballantine, 1993

Acknowledgments

This book is written in "fairy tale," the psychic mother tongue of my childhood families. In this idiom, I write about "a father," "an old man," "a child," "a tree," "a field." As in fairy tales, many of my foster family members lived in a time and a place that now exists only in memory: that war that was senselessly called the European "theatre," and also the rich but harsh life of the rural north woods in the late 1940s and 1950s.

To write of these times, I have drawn upon the Magyar love of the lyric line that I learned as a child—the simple rhythm of the story that holds together our songs, our great poems, our epics, and the chants of our family *gyógyítók,* healers and prayermakers.

For this lexicon, I am in part indebted to my dear foster parents, Joszéf and Márushka, and to their eighteen brothers and sisters, of whom Uncle Zovár was one of many closest to me. All these—including their spouses and their parents, as well as our loved ones who were murdered in wars of various kinds and those who died in epidemics—bring the total of my elders in this family to sixty-two souls.

Ten elders, who are now in their eighties and nineties, still miraculously live. They, and the myriad others who are resting in spirit now, are as vital to me as ever, and I laud, cherish, and thank them. They are truly the last of their kind on the face of this earth.

Appreciation also to Tom Grady, who understood that to children, all uncles are giants. To Kip Kotzen for his many kindnesses to me. I have been greatly assisted by the everyday love and patience of Bogie, T. J., Juan, Lucy, Virginia, Cherie, Charlie, and Lois. They all have my gratitude in return. Especially, I thank Ned Leavitt, who, it can be said fairly, has moved both earth and heaven.

CLARISSA PINKOLA ESTÉS, PH.D., INTERNATIONALLY ACCLAIMED poet, scholar, diplomate Jungian psychoanalyst, certified by and a senior member of the International Association of Analytical Psychology, Zurich, Switzerland, is also a *cantadora* (keeper of the old stories) in the Hispanic tradition. Dr. Estés's work is known worldwide for ground-breaking explorations into the nature of the psyche through the use of mythos, fairy tales, poetics, and psychoanalytic commentary. She credits a good deal of what has been called her "infinitely rich" and "one-of-a-kind voice" to having been immersed since childhood in the old and demanding oral traditions handed down to her "day by day, task by task, test by test, prayer by prayer, story by story" by her immigrant and refugee family elders, both Magyar and *Mexicano*.

Dr. Estés is former executive director of the C. G. Jung Center for Education and Research in the United States. Her doctorate is in inter-cultural studies and clinical psychology, and she has taught and prac-ticed privately for twenty-five years.

Her other published works include *The Gift of Story* and *Women Who Run with the Wolves: Myths and Stories of the Wild Woman Archetype,* published in eighteen languages worldwide.

She is the author of an eleven-volume series of bestselling audio works and a twelve-part live performance series, *Theatre of the Imagination,* broadcast on National Public Radio and Pacifica Networks across America and Canada.

A lifetime activist, she founded and directs the C. P. Estés Guadalupe Foundation, which has as one of its nascent missions the broadcasting of strengthening stories, via shortwave radio, to trouble spots throughout the world. For her lifelong social activism and writing, she is the re-cipient of the *Las Primeras* Award from MANA, The National Latina Foundation in Washington, D.C.; the 1994 recipient of The President's Medal for social justice from The Union Institute; the first recipient of the annual Joseph Campbell festival "Keeper of the Lore" Award; a winner of the Associated Catholic Church Press Award for Writing, and the recipient of The Gradiva Award 1995 from the National Associa-tion for the Advancement of Psychoanalysis, New York.

Dr. Estés is married and has three grown children. She is a lifetime member of *La Sociedad de Guadalupe.*